CLOCKWORK

—or *All Wound Up*—

Also by Philip Pullman

THE FIREWORK-MAKER'S DAUGHTER
with AFTER WORDS™

illustrated by Susan Gallagher

CLOCKWORK

—or *All Wound Up*—

PHILIP PULLMAN

with illustrations by
Leonid Gore

SCHOLASTIC INC.
New York Toronto London Auckland Sydney
Mexico City New Delhi Hong Kong Buenos Aires

ISBN 0-590-12998-8

All rights reserved. Published by Scholastic Inc., by arrangement with
Transworld Publishers Ltd. SCHOLASTIC, APPLE PAPERBACKS,
the LANTERN LOGO, and associated logos are trademarks
and/or registered trademarks of Scholastic Inc.

12 11 10 9 8 7 6 5 4 3 2 1   6 7 8 9 10 11/0

Printed in the U.S.A.   40

First Scholastic After Words printing, June 2006

Arthur A. Levine Books hardcover edition designed by David Saylor,
published by Arthur A. Levine Books,
an imprint of Scholastic Inc.,
October 1998.

The stars move still, time runs, the clock will strike,

The devil will come, and Faustus must be damn'd. . . .

CHRISTOPHER MARLOWE, *Dr. Faustus*

CONTENTS

A Note About Clocks   *ix*

PART ONE   *1*

PART TWO   *49*

PART THREE   *75*

Index of Illustrations   *109*

A NOTE ABOUT CLOCKS

IN THE OLD DAYS, when this story took place, time used to run by clockwork. Real clockwork, I mean, springs and cogwheels and gears and pendulums and so on. When you took it apart you could see how it worked, and how to put it together again. Nowadays time runs by electricity and vibrating crystals of quartz and goodness knows what else. You can even buy a watch that's powered by a solar panel, and sets itself several times a day by picking up a radio signal, and never runs a second late. Clocks and watches like that might as well work by witchcraft for all the sense I can make of them.

Real clockwork is quite mysterious enough. Take a spring, for instance, like the mainspring of an alarm clock. It's made of tempered steel, with an edge that's sharp enough to draw blood. If you play about with it carelessly it'll spring up and strike at you like a snake, and put out your eye. Or take a weight, the kind of iron weight that drives the mighty clocks they have in church towers. If your head were under that weight, and if the weight fell, it would dash out your brains on the floor.

But with the help of a few gears and pins, and a little balance wheel oscillating to and fro or a pendulum swinging from side to side, the strength of the spring and the power of the weight are led harmlessly through the clock to drive the hands.

And once you've wound up a clock, there's

something frightful in the way it keeps on going at its own relentless pace. Its hands move steadily round the dial as if they had a mind of their own. Tick-tock, tick-tock! Bit by bit they move, and tick us steadily on toward the grave.

Some stories are like that. Once you've wound them up, nothing will stop them; they move on forward till they reach their destined end, and no matter how much the characters would like to change their fate, they can't. This is one of those stories. And now that it's all wound up, we can begin.

Part One

The White Horse Tavern

Once upon a time (when time ran by clockwork) a strange event took place in a little German town. Actually, it was a series of events, all fitting together like the parts of a clock, and although each person saw a different part, no one saw the whole of it; but here it is, as well as I can tell it.

It began on a winter's evening, when the towns-folk were gathering in the White Horse Tavern. The snow was blowing down from the mountains, and the wind was making the bells shift restlessly in the church tower. The windows were steamed up, the stove was blazing brightly, Putzi the old black cat was snoozing on the hearth; and the air was full of the rich smells of sausage and sauerkraut, of tobacco and beer. Gretl the little barmaid, the landlord's daughter, was hurrying to and fro with foaming mugs and steaming plates.

The door opened, and fat white flakes of snow swirled in, to faint away into water as they met the heat of the parlor. The incomers, Herr Ringelmann the clockmaker and his apprentice Karl, stamped their boots and shook the snow off their greatcoats.

"It's Herr Ringelmann!" said the Burgomaster. "Well, old friend, come and drink some beer with me! And a mug for young what's-his-name, your apprentice. It's your day of glory tomorrow, my boy!"

Karl nodded his thanks and went to sit by

himself in a corner. His expression was dark and gloomy.

"What's the matter with young thingamajig?" said the Burgomaster. "He looks as if he's swallowed a thundercloud."

"Oh, I shouldn't worry," said the old clockmaker, sitting down at the table with his friends. "He's anxious about tomorrow. His apprenticeship is coming to an end, you see."

"Ah, of course," said the Burgomaster. It was the custom that when a clockmaker's apprentice finished his period of service, he made a new figure for the great clock of Glockenheim. "So we're to have a new piece of clockwork in the tower! Well, I look forward to seeing it tomorrow."

"I remember when my apprenticeship came to an end," said Herr Ringelmann. "I couldn't sleep for thinking about what would happen when my

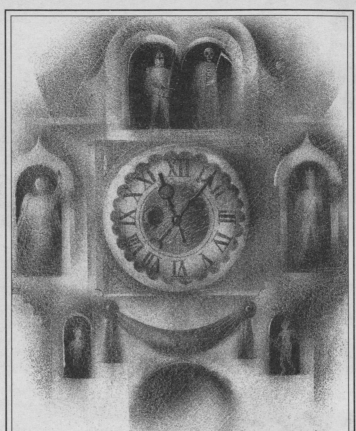

The great clock of Glockenheim was the most amazing piece of mechanism in the whole of Germany. There were over a hundred figures altogether.

figure came out of the clock. Supposing I hadn't counted the cogs properly? Supposing the spring was too stiff? Supposing—oh, a thousand things go through your mind. It's a heavy responsibility."

"Maybe so, but I've never seen the lad look so gloomy before," said someone else. "And he's not a cheerful fellow at the best of times."

It seemed to the other drinkers that Herr Ringelmann himself was a little downhearted, but he raised his mug with the rest of them and changed the conversation to another topic.

"I hear young Fritz the novelist is going to read us his new story tonight," he said.

"So I believe," said the Burgomaster. "I hope it's not as terrifying as the last one he read to us. D'you know, I woke three times that night and found my hair on end, just thinking about it!"

"I don't know if it's more frightening hearing them here in the parlor, or reading them later on your own," said another customer.

"It's worse on your own, believe me," said yet another. "You can feel the ghostly fingers creeping up your spine, and even when you know what's going to happen next, you can't help jumping when it does."

Then they argued about whether it was more terrifying to hear a ghost story when you didn't know what was going to happen (because it took you by surprise) or when you did (because there was the suspense of waiting for it). They all enjoyed ghost stories, and Fritz's in particular, for he was a talented storyteller.

The subject of their conversation, Fritz the writer himself, was a cheerful-looking young man who had been eating his supper at the other end of the parlor. He joked with the landlord, he laughed with his neighbors, and when he'd finished he called for another mug of beer, gathered up the untidy pile of manuscript pages beside his plate, and went to talk to Karl.

"Hello, old boy," he said cheerfully. "All set for tomorrow? I'm looking forward to it! What are you going to show us?"

Karl scowled and turned away.

"The artistic temperament," said the landlord wisely. "Drink up your beer, and have another on the house, in honor of tomorrow."

"Put poison in, and I'll drink it then," muttered Karl.

"What?" said Fritz, who could hardly believe his ears. The two of them were sitting right at the end of the bar, and Fritz moved so as to turn his back on the rest of the company and speak to Karl in private. "What's the matter, old fellow?" he went on quietly. "You've been working at your masterpiece for months! Surely you're not worried about it? It can't fail!"

Karl looked at him with a face full of savage bitterness.

"I haven't made a figure," he muttered. "I couldn't do it. I've failed, Fritz. When the clock chimes ten tomorrow, the mechanism will bring all the figures out in a procession, and everyone will be looking up to see what I've done. But nothing will come out, nothing. . . ." He groaned softly, and turned away. "I can't face them!" he went on. "I should go and throw myself off the tower now and have done with it!"

"Oh, come on, don't talk like that!" said Fritz, who had never seen his friend so bitter. "You must have a word with old Herr Ringelmann—ask his advice—tell him you've hit a snag—he's a decent old fellow, he'll help you out!"

"You don't understand," said Karl passionately. "Everything's so easy for you! You just sit at your desk and put pen to paper, and stories come pouring out! You don't know what it is to sweat and strain for hours on end with no ideas at all, or to struggle with materials that break and tools that go blunt, or to tear your hair out trying to find a new variation on the same old theme—I tell you, Fritz, it's a wonder I haven't blown my brains out long before this! Well, it won't be long now. Tomorrow morning you can all laugh at me. Karl the failure. Karl the hopeless. Karl the first apprentice to fail in hundreds of years of clockmaking. I don't care. I shall be lying at the bottom of the river, under the ice."

Fritz had had to stop himself from interrupting when Karl spoke about the difficulty of working. Stories are just as hard as clocks to put together, and they can go wrong just as easily—as we shall see with Fritz's own story in a page or two. Still, Fritz was an optimist, and Karl was a pessimist, and that makes all the difference in the world.

Putzi the cat, waking from his snooze on the hearth, came and rubbed his back against Karl's legs. Karl kicked him savagely away.

"Steady on," said Fritz.

But Karl only scowled. He drank deeply and wiped his mouth with the back of his hand before banging the mug on the counter and calling for more. Gretl, the young barmaid, looked anxiously at Fritz because she was only a child, and wasn't sure whether she should be serving someone in Karl's condition.

"Give him some more," said Fritz. "He's not drunk, poor fellow, he's unhappy. I'll keep an eye on him, don't you worry."

So Gretl poured some more beer for Karl, and the clockmaker's apprentice scowled and turned away. Fritz was worried about him, but he couldn't stay there any longer, because the patrons were calling for him.

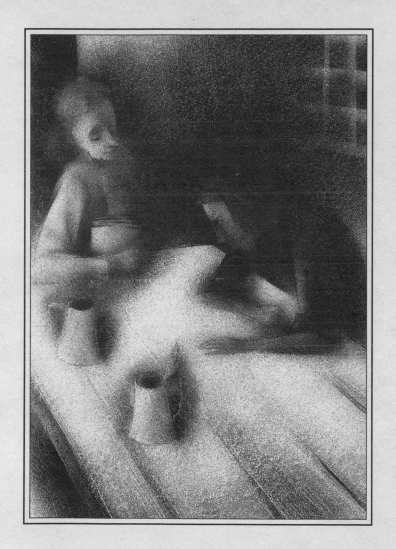

Karl only scowled.

"Come on, Fritz! Where's that story?"

"Sing for your supper! Come on! We're all waiting!"

"What's it about this time, eh? Skeletons, or ghosts?"

"I hope it's a nice bloody murder!"

"No, I hear he's got something quite different for us this time. Something quite new."

"I've got a feeling it's going to be more horrible than anything we could imagine," said old Johann the woodcutter.

While the drinkers ordered more mugs of beer to see them through the story, and filled their pipes and settled themselves comfortably, Fritz gathered up his manuscript and took up his place by the stove.

To tell the truth, Fritz was less comfortable himself than he had ever been before at one of these storytelling evenings, because of what Karl had just told him, and because of the theme of his story—of the start of it, anyway. But after all it wasn't about Karl. The subject was really quite different.

(There was another private reason for Fritz to be nervous. The fact was, he hadn't actually finished the story. He'd written the start all right, and it was terrific, but he hadn't been able to think of an ending. He was just going to wind up the story, set it going, and make up the end when he got there. As I said just now, he was an optimist.)

"We're all ready and waiting," said the Burgomaster. "I'm looking forward to this story, even if it does make my hair stand on end. What's it called?"

"It's called—" said Fritz, with a nervous glance at Karl—"it's called 'Clockwork.'"

"Ah! Very appropriate!" cried old Herr Ringelmann. "Did you hear that, Karl? This is a story in your honor, my boy!"

Karl scowled and looked down at the floor.

"No, no," said Fritz hastily, "this story isn't about Karl, or the clock in our town—no, not at all. It's quite different. It just happens to be called 'Clockwork.'"

"Well, set it going," said someone. "We're all ready."

So Fritz cleared his throat and arranged his papers and began to read.

FRITZ'S STORY

"I WONDER IF ANY OF YOU remember the extraordinary business at the palace a few years ago? They tried to hush it up, but some details came out, and a bizarre mystery it was, too. It seems that Prince Otto had taken his young son Florian hunting, together with an old friend of the royal family, Baron Stelgratz. It was the dead of winter—just like now. They'd set off in a sledge for the hunting lodge up in the mountains, well wrapped up against the cold, and they weren't expected back for a week or so.

"Well, what should happen but that only two nights later, the sentry on duty at the palace gate saw a commotion down the road, and heard the whinnying of horses—whinnying in panic—making a terrible racket; and it looked, though he couldn't be sure, as if a sledge was being driven toward the palace by a madman.

"The sentry raised the alarm and called for lights, and when the sledge got close enough, they could see that it was the royal sledge, the very one the Prince had set off in only three nights before. It was hurtling up the road behind those terrified horses, and it wasn't going to stop; and the sergeant of the guard gave orders to drag the palace gates open quickly before it crashed.

"They got them open just in time. The sledge rushed through, and then drove round and round the courtyard, for the horses were mad with fear and couldn't stop. The poor beasts were covered with foam and their eyes were rolling, and the sledge would be going round that courtyard still if one of the runners hadn't caught on a mounting block and turned the whole thing over.

"Out fell the driver, and out fell a bundle in the back of the sledge. A servant hastened to pick it up, and found little Prince Florian wrapped in a fur rug, safe and warm and half-asleep.

"But as for the driver . . .

"Well, as soon as the sentries came close, they saw who it was. It was none other than Prince Otto himself, stark dead, as cold as ice, with his eyes wide and staring ahead of him, his left hand

...the horses were mad with fear...

gripping the reins so tight they had to be cut loose, and (this was the strangest part) his right hand still moving, lashing the whip up and down, up and down, up and down.

"They covered him up so the Princess, his wife, wouldn't see him, and took little Prince Florian to her to prove he was alive and well; because he was their only child.

"But what was to be done with Prince Otto? They took his body into the palace and sent for the Royal Physician, a worthy old man who'd studied in Heidelberg and Paris and Bologna, and published a treatise on the location of the soul; he'd studied geology, hydrology, and physiology, but he'd never seen anything like this before. A dead body that wouldn't keep still! Imagine that! Stretched out icy cold on a marble slab, with its right arm lashing and lashing and lashing with no sign that it was ever going to stop.

"The Physician locked the door to keep the servants out, brought the lamp closer, and bent low to look, whereupon his eye was caught by something in the clumsy arrangement of the clothes. So, avoiding that lashing right arm, he carefully unfastened the cloak and the fur coat and the underjacket and the shirt, and laid the Prince's chest bare.

"And there it was: a gash across his breast just over the heart, crudely sewn up with a dozen stitches. The Physician got his scissors and snipped them away, and then he nearly fainted with surprise, because when he opened the wound, there was no heart there. Instead there was a little piece of clockwork: just a few cogs and springs and a balance wheel, attached in subtle ways to the Prince's veins and tick-tick-ticking away merrily, in perfect time with the lashing of his arm.

"Well, you can imagine how the Physician

crossed himself and took a sip of brandy to calm his nerves. Who wouldn't? Then he carefully cut the attachments and lifted out the clockwork, and as he did, the arm fell still, just like that."

As he got to that point in his story, Fritz paused for a sip of beer, and to see how his audience was taking it. The silence in the tavern was profound. Every single customer was sitting so still they might have been dead themselves, except for their wide eyes and expressions of tense excitement. He had never had such a success!

He turned the page and read on:

FRITZ'S STORY *(continued)*

"WELL, THE PHYSICIAN sewed up Prince Otto's wound, and let it be known that the Prince had died of apoplexy. The servants who'd carried the body in thought differently; they knew a dead man when they saw one, even if his arm was moving. At any rate, the official version was that Prince Otto had suffered a contusion of the brain, and that his love for his son had kept him alive just long enough to drive him safely home. He was buried with a good deal of ceremony, and everyone was in mourning for six months.

"As for what had happened to Baron Stelgratz, the other member of the hunting party, no one could guess. The whole affair was shrouded in mystery.

"But the Royal Physician had an idea. There was one man who might be able to explain what had happened, and that was the great Dr. Kalmenius of Schatzberg, of whom very few people had heard; but those who did know of him said he was the cleverest man in Europe. For making clockwork, he had no equal, not even our good Herr Ringelmann. He could make intricate pieces of calculating apparatus that worked out the positions of all the stars and the planets, and answer any mathematical question.

"Dr. Kalmenius could have made his fortune if he'd wanted to, but he wasn't interested in fortune or in fame. He was interested in something far deeper than that. He would spend hours sitting in graveyards, contemplating the mysteries of life and death. Some said he experimented on dead bodies. Others said he was in league with the powers of darkness. No one knew for certain. But one thing they did know was that he used to walk about at night, pulling behind him a little sledge containing whatever secret matter he was working on at the time.

"What did he look like, this philosopher of the night? He was very tall and thin, with a prominent

There was something uncanny about Dr. Kalmenius's clockwork. He made little figures that sang, and spoke, and played chess, and shot tiny arrows from tiny bows, and played the harpsichord as well as Mozart. You can see some of his clockwork figures today in the museum at Schatzberg, but they don't work anymore. It's odd, because all the parts are in place, and in perfect order, and they should work; but they don't. It's almost as if they had . . . died.

nose and jaw. His eyes blazed like coals in caverns of darkness. His hair was long and gray, and he wore a black cloak with a loose hood like that of a monk; he had a harsh, grating voice, and his expression was full of savage curiosity.

"And that was the man who—"

Fritz stopped.

He swallowed, and his eyes moved to the door. Everyone followed his gaze. The parlor had never been so still. No one moved, no one dared to breathe, for the latch was lifting.

The door slowly opened.

On the threshold stood a man in a long black cloak with a loose hood like a monk's. His gray hair hung down on either side of his face: a long, narrow face with a prominent nose and jaw, and eyes that looked like burning coals in caverns of darkness.

Oh, the silence as he stepped inside! Every

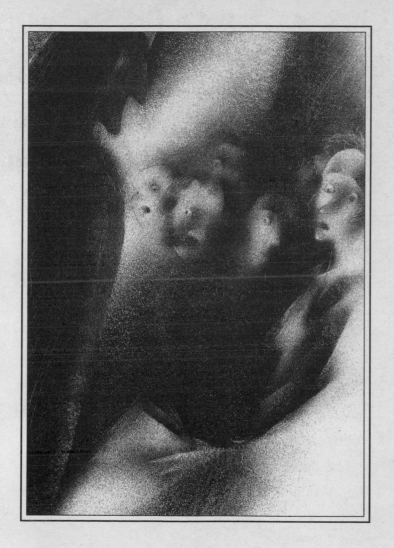

On the threshold stood a man . . .

single person in the parlor was gaping, mouth open, eyes wide; and when they saw what the stranger was pulling behind him—a little sledge with something wrapped in canvas—more than one crossed themselves and stood up in fear.

The stranger bowed.

"Dr. Kalmenius, of Schatzberg, at your service," he said, in a harsh, grating voice. "I have come a long way tonight, and I am cold. A glass of brandy!"

The landlord poured it hastily. The stranger drained it at once and held out his glass for more. Still nobody moved.

"So silent?" said Dr. Kalmenius, looking around mockingly. "One might think one had arrived among the dead!"

The Burgomaster swallowed hard and got to his feet.

"I beg your pardon, Doctor—er—Kalmenius,

but the fact is that—"

And he looked at Fritz, who was staring at Dr. Kalmenius with horror. The young man was as pale as the paper in his hand. His eyes were nearly starting from his head, his hands trembled like leaves, and a ghastly sweat had broken out on his forehead.

"Yes, my good sir?" said Dr. Kalmenius.

"I—I—" said Fritz, and swallowed convulsively.

The Burgomaster intervened: "The fact is that our young friend is a writer of stories, Doctor, and he was reading us one of his tales when you arrived."

"Ah! How delightful!" said Dr. Kalmenius. "I should greatly enjoy hearing the rest of your story, young sir. Please don't feel inhibited by my presence—carry on as if I weren't here at all."

A little cry broke from Fritz's throat. With a

sudden movement he crumpled all his sheets of paper together and thrust them into the stove, where they blazed up high.

"I beg you," he cried, "have nothing to do with this man!"

And like someone who has seen the Devil, he ran out of the inn as fast as he could.

Dr. Kalmenius broke into a wild and mocking laugh, and at that, several other good citizens followed Fritz's example, left their pipes and their mugs of beer, grabbed their coats and hats, and were off, not even daring to look the stranger in the eye.

Herr Ringelmann and the Burgomaster were almost the last to leave. The old clockmaker thought he should say something to a fellow craftsman, but his tongue was mute; and the Burgomaster thought he should either welcome the eminent Dr. Kalmenius or send him on his way, but his nerve failed. The two old men took their sticks and hurried away as fast as they could.

Little Gretl was clinging to her father, the landlord, watching it all with wide eyes.

"Well!" said Dr. Kalmenius. "You keep early hours in this town. I will take another glass of brandy."

The landlord poured with a shaking hand, and ushered Gretl out, for this was no company for a child.

Dr. Kalmenius drained the brandy at once, and called for yet another.

"And perhaps this gentleman will join me," he said, turning to the corner of the bar.

For there sat Karl still. In the rush of all the other customers to leave, he had not moved. He turned his glowering face, now flushed with drink and sullen with self-hatred, to glare at the stranger, but he could not meet those mocking eyes, and he dropped his gaze to the floor.

"Bring a glass for my companion," said Dr. Kalmenius to the landlord, "and then you may leave us."

The landlord put the bottle and another glass on the bar, and fled. Only five minutes before, the parlor had been full to bursting; but now Dr. Kalmenius and Karl were alone, and the inn was so quiet that Karl could hear the whisper of flames in the stove, and the ticking of the old clock in the corner, even over the beating of his own heart.

Dr. Kalmenius poured some brandy and pushed the glass along the bar. Karl said nothing. He bore the stranger's stare for nearly a minute, and then he banged his fist on the counter and cried:

"God damn you, what do you want?"

"Of you, sir? I want nothing from you."

"You came here on purpose to jeer at me!"

"To jeer at you? Come, come, we have better

clowns than you in Schatzberg. Should I come all this way to laugh at a young man whose face shows nothing but unhappiness? Come, drink up! Look cheerful! It is your morning of triumph tomorrow!"

Karl groaned and turned away, but Dr. Kalmenius's mocking voice continued:

"Yes, the unveiling of a new figure for the famous clock of Glockenheim is an important occasion. Do you know, I tried to find a bed in five different inns before I came here, and they were all full up. Visitors from all over Germany—gentlemen and ladies—craftsmen, clockmakers, experts in all kinds of machinery—all come to see your new figure, your masterpiece! Isn't that something to be joyful about? Drink, my friend, drink!"

Karl snatched the glass and swallowed the fiery liquor.

"There won't be a new figure," he muttered.

"What's this?"

"I said there won't be a new figure. I haven't made one. I couldn't. I wasted all my time, and when it was too late I found I couldn't do it. There you are. Now you can laugh at me. Go on."

"Oh, dear, dear," said Dr. Kalmenius solemnly. "Laugh? I wouldn't dream of it. I've come here to help you."

"What? You? How?"

Dr. Kalmenius smiled. It was like a flame suddenly breaking out of an ash-covered log, and Karl recoiled. The old man came closer.

"You see," he said, "I think you may have overlooked the philosophical implications of our craft. You know how to regulate a watch and repair a church clock, but had you ever considered that our lives are clockwork too?"

"I don't understand," said Karl.

"We can control the future, my boy, just as we wind up the mechanism in a clock. Say to yourself: I will win that race—I will come first—and you wind up the future like clockwork. The world has no choice but to obey! Can the hands of that old clock in the corner decide to stop? Can the spring in your watch decide to wind itself up and run backward? No! They have no choice. And nor has the future, once you have wound it up."

"Impossible," said Karl, who was feeling more and more light-headed.

"Oh, but it's easy! What would you like? Wealth? A beautiful bride? Wind up the future, my friend! Say what you want, and it will be yours! Fame, power, riches—what would you like?"

"You know very well what I want!" cried Karl. "I want a figure for the clock! Something to show for all the time I should have spent in making it! Anything to avoid the shame I'll feel tomorrow!"

"Nothing could be easier," said Dr. Kalmenius. "You spoke—and there is what you wished for."

He pointed to the little sledge he'd pulled behind him into the parlor. The runners stood in a puddle of melted snow, and the canvas cover was damp.

"What is it?" said Karl, who had suddenly become very afraid.

"Uncover it! Take off the canvas!"

Karl got unsteadily to his feet and slowly untied the rope holding the cover down. Then he pulled the canvas off.

In the sledge was the most perfect piece of metal sculpture he had ever seen. It was the figure of a knight in armor, made of gleaming, silvery metal, holding a sharp sword. Karl gasped at the detail, and walked around looking at it from all angles. Every piece of armor plating was polished

Karl gasped at the detail . . .

and shiny and tightly riveted to the next, and as for the sword—

He touched it and drew his hand back at once, looking at the blood running down his fingers.

"It's like a razor," he said.

"Only the best will do for Sir Ironsoul," said Dr. Kalmenius.

"Sir Ironsoul. . . . What a piece of work! Oh, if this were in the tower among the other figures, my name would be made forever!" said Karl bitterly. "And how does he move? What does he do? He *does* work by clockwork, I suppose? Or is there some kind of goblin in there? A spirit or a devil of some kind?"

With a smooth whirr and a ticking of delicate machinery, the figure began to move. The knight raised his sword and turned his helmeted head to look for Karl, and then stepped off the sledge and moved toward him.

"No! What's he doing?" said Karl in alarm, backing away.

Sir Ironsoul kept going. Karl moved aside, but the figure turned too, and before Karl could dodge away he was pinned in the corner, with the little knight's sword moving closer and closer.

"What's he doing? That sword is sharp—stop it, Doctor! Make it stop!"

Dr. Kalmenius whistled three or four bars of a simple, haunting little tune, and Sir Ironsoul fell still. The point of the sword was right at Karl's throat.

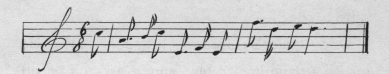

The apprentice eased his way past the figure and sank onto a chair, weak with fear.

"What—who—how did it start? This is uncanny! Did you set it off?"

"Oh, I didn't start him," said Dr. Kalmenius. "You did."

"I did? How?"

"It was something you said. His mechanism is so delicate, so perfectly balanced, that one word, and one word alone, will start him moving. And he's such a clever little fellow! Once he's heard that word, he won't rest until his sword is in the throat that uttered it."

"What word?" said Karl fearfully. "What did I say? Clockwork . . . goblin . . . move . . . work . . . spirit . . . devil—"

Once again Sir Ironsoul began to move. He turned around implacably, found Karl, and set off toward him. The apprentice was out of his chair in a flash and cowering in the corner.

"That was it!" he cried. "Stop it again, please, Doctor!"

Dr. Kalmenius whistled once more, and the figure stopped.

"What is that tune?" said Karl. "Why does he stop for that?"

"It's a little tune called 'The Flowers of Lapland,'" said Dr. Kalmenius. "He likes that, bless him. He stands still to listen to it, and that tips his balance wheel the other way, and then he stops. What a marvel! What a piece of work!"

"I'm afraid of him."

"Oh, come, come! Afraid of a little tin man who likes a pretty tune?"

"It's uncanny. It's not like a machine at all. I don't like it."

"Well, that's a great shame. What will you do without him tomorrow? I shall be watching with great interest."

"No, no!" said Karl in anguish. "I didn't mean. . . . Oh, I don't know what I mean!"

"Do you want him?"

"Yes. No!" cried Karl, beating his fists together. "I don't know. Yes!"

"Then he is yours," said Dr. Kalmenius. "You have wound up the future, my boy! It has already begun to tick!"

And before Karl could change his mind, the clockwork maker gathered his long cloak around him, swept the hood up over his head, and vanished out the door with his sledge.

Karl ran to the door after him, but the snow was so thick that he could see nothing. Dr. Kalmenius had vanished.

Karl turned back into the parlor and sat down weakly. The little figure stood perfectly still, with its sword upraised, and its blank metal face gazing at the young apprentice.

"He wasn't a man," Karl muttered. "No man could make this. He was an evil spirit! He was the Dev—"

He clapped his hands over his mouth and looked in terror at Sir Ironsoul, who stood motionless.

"I nearly said it!" Karl whispered to himself. "I mustn't ever forget—and the tune! How does it go? If I can remember that, I'll be safe. . . . "

He tried to whistle it, but his mouth was too dry; he tried to hum it, but his voice was shaking. He held out his hands and looked at them. They were trembling like dry leaves.

"Perhaps if I have another drink . . . " he said.

He poured some more brandy, splashing most of it on the counter before he got some in the glass. He swallowed it quickly.

"That's better. Well, after all, I could put him in the clock. And if I bolted him to the frame, he'd be safe enough. He wouldn't be able to get out of that, no matter what words anyone said. . . . "

He looked around him fearfully. The parlor was as silent as the grave. Then he lifted the curtain and peered through the window, but there was not a single light in the town square. Everyone in the world seemed to have gone to bed, and the only beings awake were the clockmaker's apprentice and the little silvery figure with the sword.

"Yes, I'll do it!" he said.

So he threw the canvas over Sir Ironsoul, hastily pulled on his coat and hat, and hurried to the town square to unlock the tower and prepare the clock.

Now as it happened, there was one other person awake, and that was Gretl, the landlord's little daughter. She couldn't sleep at all, and the reason for that was Fritz's story. There was one thing she couldn't get out of her mind. It wasn't the clock-work in the dead Prince's breast; it wasn't the

horses foaming with terror or the dead driver behind them; it was the young Prince Florian.

She thought: poor little boy, to travel home in
that frightful way! She tried to imagine what ter-
rors he must have faced, alone in the sledge with
his dead father, and she shivered under her blan-
kets, and wished that she could comfort him.

And because she couldn't sleep, she thought
she'd go down and sit by the stove in the parlor for
a while, because her bed was cold. So she wrapped
a blanket around her shoulders and tiptoed down
the stairs just as the great clock in the tower was
chiming midnight. There was no one in the parlor,
of course, except for the cat, and the lamp was
burning low, so she didn't notice the canvas-
covered figure in the corner, and sat down to warm
her hands at the stove.

"What a strange story that was going to be!" she
said to Putzi, stroking his ears. "I'm not sure that

people ought to tell stories like that. I don't mind ghosts and skeletons, but I think Fritz went too far that time. And didn't everyone jump when the old man came in! It was as if Fritz conjured him up out of nothing. Like Dr. Faust, conjuring up the Devil...."

The sheet of canvas fell softly to the floor, and the little metal figure turned his head, raised his sword, and began to move toward her.

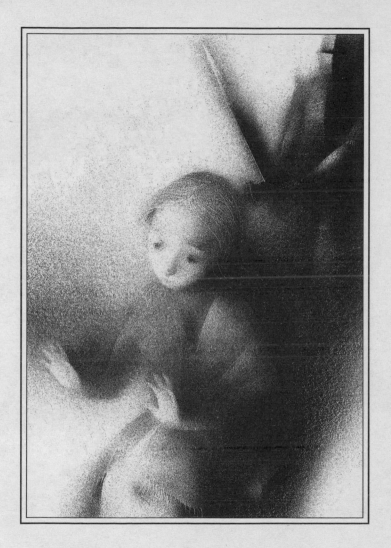

The sheet of canvas fell softly to the floor . . .

Part Two

Prince Otto and Princess Mariposa

When Prince Otto married his Princess Mariposa, the whole city rejoiced: fireworks were lit in the public gardens, bands played all night in the ballrooms, and flags and banners waved from every rooftop.

"At last we'll have an heir!" the people said, for they had been afraid that the dynasty would come to an end.

But time went by, and more time, and no child came to Prince Otto and Princess Mariposa. They sought the opinions of the finest doctors, but still no child came. They made a pilgrimage to Rome to seek the blessing of the Pope, but still no child came. Finally, as Princess Mariposa stood at the palace window, she heard the chiming of the cathedral clock and said, "I wish I had a child as sound as a bell and as true as a clock"; and when she had said those words, she felt her heart lift.

And before the year was out, she did have a child. But alas for her and for everyone, her labor was hard and painful, and when the baby had taken one breath in this world, he could take no more, and he died in the arms of the nurse. Princess Mariposa knew nothing of that, for she was in a dreadful swoon, and no one could say whether she would live or die. As for Prince Otto, he was nearly out of his mind with fury. He snatched the dead child from the nurse's arms and said, "I will have an heir, come what may!"

He ran down to the stables and ordered the grooms to saddle his fastest horse, and, with the dead child clasped to his breast, he galloped away.

Where was he going? North, and farther north, until he came to the workshop of Dr. Kalmenius, near the silver mines of Schatzberg. There it was that the great clockwork-maker created his wonders, from the celestial clocks that told the position of every planet for the next twenty-five thousand years, to the little figures that danced and rode miniature ponies and shot tiny arrows and played the harpsichord.

"Well?" said Dr. Kalmenius.

Prince Otto stood in his riding cloak with the snow still white on his shoulders, and held out the body of his child.

"Make me another child!" he said. "My son is dead, and his mother lies between life and death! Dr. Kalmenius, I command you to make me a child of clockwork who will not die!"

Even Prince Otto, in his madness, didn't believe that a clockwork toy could resemble a living child; but the silver they mined in Schatzberg was not the same as other metals. It was malleable and soft and lustrous, with a bloom on it like that on a butterfly's wing. As for the great clockwork-maker, the task was a challenge to his artistry that he couldn't resist, and so, while Prince Otto buried the dead child, Dr. Kalmenius set to work to make the new one. He smelted the ore and refined the silver, and beat it into a subtle thinness; he spun gold into filaments finer than spiders' silk, and attached each one separately to the little head; he cast and filed and tempered, he soldered and riveted and bolted, he timed and adjusted and regulated, until the little mainspring was tight and the little escapement on its jeweled bearings was ticking back and forth with perfect accuracy; and

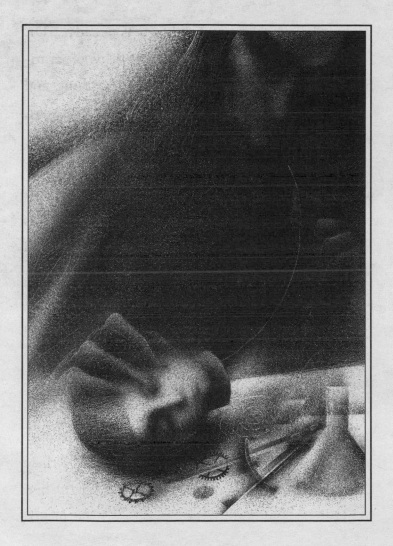

He spun gold into filaments finer than spiders' silk . . .

when the clockwork child was ready, Dr. Kalmenius gave him to Prince Otto, who scrutinized him carefully. The baby was breathing and moving and smiling and even, by some secret art, warm. In every way he looked exactly like the child who had died. Prince Otto wrapped his cloak around the baby and rode back to the palace, where he laid the child in the arms of Princess Mariposa; and the princess opened her eyes, and the joy of seeing her own child, as she thought, alive and well, brought her back from the brink of the grave. Besides, she looked so pretty with a child in her arms; she had always known she would.

They named him Florian. A year went by, two years, three, and the little boy grew up admired by everyone, happy and sturdy and clever. Prince Otto took him riding on a little pony, taught him to shoot a bow and arrow; he danced, he picked out tunes on the harpsichord; he grew stronger and bigger, more merry and lively all the time.

But in the fifth year of his life, the little prince began to show signs of a disturbing illness. There was a painful stiffness in his joints, he had a constant feeling of chill, and his face, which was normally so lively and expressive, was becoming masklike and rigid. Princess Mariposa was worried to distraction, for he no longer looked nearly so handsome next to her.

"Can't you do something to cure him?" she demanded of the Royal Physician.

The Physician tapped the boy's chest and looked at his tongue and felt his pulse. It was like no disease he had ever seen. If he hadn't known the prince was a little boy, he'd have said he was seizing up like a rusty clock; but he could hardly say that to Princess Mariposa.

"Nothing to worry about," he said. "It's a

condition known as inflammatory oxidosis. Give him two spoonfuls of cod-liver oil three times a day, and rub his chest with oil of lavender."

The only one to suspect the truth was his father, and so Prince Otto set off once again for the mines of Schatzberg, and knocked at the door of Dr. Kalmenius's workshop.

"Well?" said the clockwork-maker.

"Prince Florian is ill," said Prince Otto. "What can we do?"

He described the symptoms, and Dr. Kalmenius shrugged his shoulders.

"It's in the nature of clockwork to run down," was the answer. "His mainspring was bound to weaken, his escapement to become clogged with dust. I can tell you what will happen next: his skin will stiffen and crack, and split from top to bottom to reveal nothing but dead, seized-up metal inside him. He will never work again."

"But why didn't you tell me this would happen?"

"You were in such a hurry that you didn't ask."

"Can't you just wind him up?"

"Impossible."

"But what can we do?" said Prince Otto in his rage and despair. "Is there nothing that can save his life? I must have an heir! The survival of the royal family depends on it!"

"There is one thing," said Dr. Kalmenius. "He is failing because he has no heart. Find him a heart, and he will live. But I don't know where you'll find a heart in good condition that its owner is willing to part with. Besides—"

But Prince Otto had left already. He didn't stop to hear the rest of what Dr. Kalmenius was going to say. That's often the way with princes; they want instant solutions, not difficult ones that take time and care to bring about. What the great clockwork-maker had been going to say was this: "The heart that is given must also be kept." But quite possibly Prince Otto wouldn't have understood anyway.

He rode back to the palace, turning the problem over in his mind. And what a dilemma! To save his son, he had to sacrifice another human being! What could he do? And whom could he ask to make such a great sacrifice?

And then he thought of the Baron von Stelgratz.

Of course! There was no one better. Baron Stelgratz was an old, trusted adviser, a staunch friend, faithful, brave, and true. The little prince loved him, and he and the Baron used to play for hours at mock battles with Prince Florian's toy soldiers, and the good old nobleman would teach him how to handle a sword or fire a pistol, and tell him all about the animals of the forest.

The more Prince Otto thought about it, the better a choice it seemed. Baron Stelgratz would leap at the chance to give his heart for the family. Better not tell him yet, though; better wait till they were at Dr. Kalmenius's workshop; then he would see the necessity quite clearly.

When Prince Otto arrived back at the palace, he found that the little prince had gotten worse. He could hardly walk without falling over stiffly, and his voice, which had been so full of life and laughter, was becoming more and more like a music box; he said very little, but he sang the same few songs over and over. It was clear that he wouldn't last very long.

So Prince Otto went straight to the Princess, and persuaded her that a few days' hunting, some brisk exercise in the forest, would do the little child a power of good. Furthermore, he said, Baron Stelgratz would accompany them; no harm would come to Florian in the Baron's company.

So Prince Otto wrapped the little boy up well and set him in the sledge with Baron Stelgratz beside him, and off they set.

But on the way through the forest, as darkness was falling, the sledge was attacked by wolves.

Maddened by hunger, the great gray beasts poured out of the trees and sprang up at the horses. Prince Otto lashed his whip furiously, and the sledge leapt forward, with the wolves tearing after. Prince Florian sat beside the Baron, gripping the side of the sledge, and watched fearfully as the wolf pack raced closer and closer. Baron Stelgratz emptied his rifle at the pack of leaping, slavering beasts, without deterring them in the least, and the sledge bumped and swayed from side to side on the rough track. At any moment they might crash, and then they would all perish.

"Highness!" cried the Baron. "There is only one

thing to do, and I do it with all my heart!"

And the good old man threw himself off the sledge. To save his friends, he sacrificed himself.

Instantly the wild wolves turned on him and tore him to pieces, and the sledge drove on into the silent forest, leaving the snarling, howling beasts far behind.

And now what could Prince Otto do?

Drive on, was the only answer; drive on! And hope to find some lonely huntsman or woodcutter, and compensate their family later on. But not a single human being came in view. Behind Prince Otto the little child, wrapped in furs, was huddled alone on the bouncing seat of the sledge, stiffening, growing colder, changing back into a machine minute by minute. Occasionally the movement of the sledge would shake a little song out of him, but he spoke no more.

Finally they arrived at the mines of Schatzberg,

To save his friends, he sacrificed himself.

and the house of the clockwork-maker.

And there was only one solution. Prince Otto realized that he had to sacrifice himself, and he was ready. The dynasty was more important than anything else: more important than happiness, than love, than truth, than peace, than honor; far more important than his own life. Prince Otto would give up his heart, cold, fanatical, and proud as it was, for the sake of the future glory of the royal house.

"You're quite sure this is what you want?" said Dr. Kalmenius.

"Don't argue with me! Take out my heart, and put it in my child's breast! It doesn't matter if I die, as long as the dynasty lives!"

The problem now was not the heart, it was the return: how could the child drive back on his own? So, for an extra payment, Dr. Kalmenius agreed to animate the dead body of Prince Otto with a small degree of purpose—just enough to drive the sledge back to the palace.

The operation was performed. Prince Otto's heart was detached from his breast with subtle instruments and transferred into the weak and failing body of the silver boy. Instantly a bright flush of health took the place of Prince Florian's metallic pallor; his eyes opened, and a lively vigor spread through all his limbs. He was alive.

Meanwhile, Dr. Kalmenius prepared a simple piece of clockwork apparatus to put in the breast of Prince Otto. It was very crude; when it was wound up, it would make his body drive to the palace. That was all it would do. But it would do it for a long, long time. If Prince Otto's body had been taken to the other side of the world, he would have set off at once for home, though the flesh rotted and fell off his bones, and would never stop until many years later his skeleton drove the sledge into the courtyard, with the clockwork ticking in his ribs.

So Dr. Kalmenius placed the sleeping body of Prince Florian in the sledge, well wrapped up against the cold, and put the whip into the hand of his dead father, who began at once to lash and lash and lash; and the horses, foaming with terror, began their mad gallop homeward.

And a strange homecoming they had of it. You might have heard the tale of how the sledge drove in at the palace gates, and how the Royal Physician found the clockwork heart. The servants whispered about the dead man whose arm wouldn't keep still; and rumors and guesses flew through the palace and the city like shuttles in a loom, weaving a story of corpses and ghosts, of curses and devils, of death and life and clockwork. But no one knew the truth.

So time passed. They searched for the Baron;

they mourned for Prince Otto; Princess Mariposa wept very fetchingly in her widow's black; and Prince Florian grew. Five more years went by, and everyone said how handsome the little prince was, how merry and good, how lucky they were to have such a child as the heir of the family!

But as the winter of the prince's tenth year set in, the dreaded symptoms returned. Prince Florian complained of pains in his joints, of a stiffness in his arms and legs, of a constant chill; his voice lost its human expressiveness and took on the tinkling sound of a music box.

Just as before, the Royal Physician was baffled.

"He has inherited this disease from his father," he said. "There can be no question about that."

"But what disease is it?" said Princess Mariposa.

"A congenital weakness of the heart," said the Physician, sounding as if he knew. "Combined with inflammatory oxidosis. But if you remember,

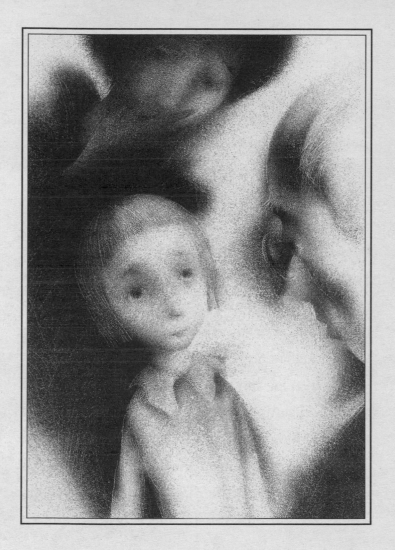

. . . the dreaded symptoms returned.

Your Highness, we cured that last time by means of healthy exercise in the forest. What Prince Florian needs is a week at the hunting lodge."

"But last time he went with his father and Baron Stelgratz, and you know what happened then!"

"Ah, medical science has advanced wonderfully in the past five years," said the Physician. "Have no fear, Your Highness. We shall arrange a hunting trip for the little prince, and he will come back glowing with health, just as he did before."

But it seemed that the courtiers had less faith in the advance of medical science than the Physician, for they all remembered what had happened last time, and none of them wanted to risk a journey through the forest even if it was to save Prince Florian. This one had gout, that one had an urgent appointment in Venice, another had to visit his aged grandmother in Berlin, and so on, and so on. There was no question of the Physician himself going: he was needed every moment at the palace, in case of an emergency. And Princess Mariposa could not possibly go, because the winter air was so bad for her complexion.

Finally, because there was no one else to do it, they called up one of the grooms and offered him ten silver pieces to take little Prince Florian to the hunting lodge.

"In advance?" the man said, because he had heard the story of what had happened before, and wanted to be sure of his money if anything went wrong.

So they gave him the silver in advance, and the groom tucked Prince Florian into the sledge and harnessed the horses. Princess Mariposa waved from the window as they drove away.

When they had gone some way into the forest, the groom thought: I don't think this lad can last another day; he looks pretty bad to me. And if I go back and tell them he's died, they're bound to punish me. On the other hand, with ten silver pieces and this sledge I can make my way over the border and set up in business on my own account. Buy a little inn, maybe find a wife and have some children of my own. Yes, that's what I'll do. There's nothing that can save this little fellow; I'm doing him a kindness, really; it's a mercy, that's what it is.

So he stopped the sledge at a crossroads and put Prince Florian out.

"Go on," the groom said, "go on, you're on your own now, I can't look after you anymore. Have a good brisk walk. Stretch your legs. Off you go."

And he drove away.

Prince Florian obediently started to walk. His legs were very stiff, and the snow lay thickly on the road, but he kept going till he turned a bend and looked down at a little town silent under the moon, where a bell in a church tower was chiming midnight.

A light was glowing in the window of an inn, and an old black cat watched from the shadows. Prince Florian struggled up to the door and opened it. Being unable to speak, he politely began to sing his one remaining song.

Part Three

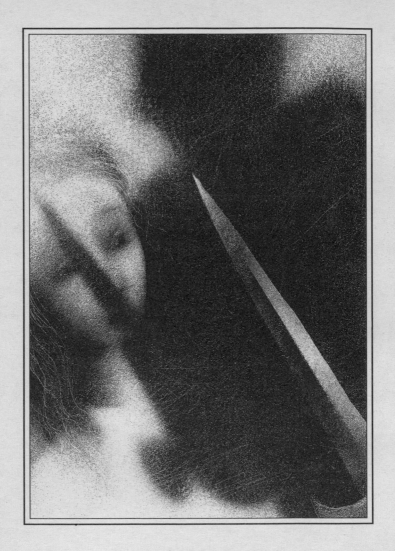

Gretl could only stare . . .

Sir Ironsoul stopped at once, with a whirr and a click. His sword was inches from Gretl's throat. The prince's song rang out sweetly through the parlor.

Gretl could only stare: in horror at Sir Ironsoul and his sword, in wonder at the prince.

"Where did you come from?" she said. "Are you the little prince in the story? I think you must be. But how cold you are! And who is this? How sharp his sword is! I don't like him at all. Oh, what must I do? I feel I'm supposed to do something, but I don't know what it is!"

There was no one to help. She was alone with the two little figures, one all malice, the other all sweetness. Gretl touched the prince's cheek gently and found it cold, but her touch awoke something in his machinery for an instant, and he turned his eyes to hers and smiled.

"Oh, you poor thing!" she cried.

He opened his lips, and sang one or two notes.

"I know what it is," said Gretl, "you're not well. And I don't like that little knight one bit, and I don't want to leave you here with him, but I know whose fault this is. It was Fritz who made the story up. If only we could find out how it finished...."

She looked at the stove, where Fritz had thrown the sheets of paper on which his story was written. She had thought they were all destroyed, but crumpled up on the floor, in the shadow, there was one piece left unburned.

She picked it up and straightened it out. It was the very page he had been reading when the stranger had come in. On it were the words:

He was very tall and thin, with a prominent nose and jaw. His eyes blazed like coals in caverns of darkness. His hair was long and gray, and he wore a black cloak with a loose hood like that of a monk; he had a harsh, grating voice, and his expression was full of savage curiosity.

And that was the man who

There was no more. The story stopped at that point.

"That was exactly when he came in!" said Gretl to herself. But there were another few words scribbled below, and peering closely, she managed to make them out.

Oh, this is impossible! How can I write an ending to this story? I'll have to make it up when I get there, and hope I do it well. If I come up with something good, the Devil can have my soul!

Gretl's eyes widened, and she bit her lip in horror. People shouldn't say things like that!

"Well," she said to herself, "he started it all off, and I'm going to make him finish it. You sit in here and keep warm, Prince Florian, if that's who you really are, and I'll go and fetch Fritz. He's the only one who can sort it out."

So she threw on her cloak and set off to the house where Fritz the storyteller had his lodging.

Meanwhile, Karl had been preparing the place in the mechanism of the great clock that was set aside for his masterpiece. Feverish with excitement, he hurried down the staircase of the clock tower and across the square to the inn. The old cat Putzi had come outside with Gretl, but he didn't like the cold and he sat on the windowsill, cleaning his ears, wondering if this man would let him in again for a snooze by the stove.

But Karl didn't notice him. He had other things than cats on his mind. He went in quietly and shut the door, and then he stopped in alarm, for there was the canvas, thrown aside, and there was Sir Ironsoul, sword upraised, on the other side of the room.

Karl's heart missed a beat. Had someone else come in and disturbed the little knight? There was no one dead, at least; but why had the figure moved? Karl looked around, and then he saw the little prince sitting politely in his chair, watching him. A thousand strange fears ran over his skin.

Karl opened his mouth to speak, and then realized that the child wasn't alive after all. It was another clockwork figure like Sir Ironsoul! And a far finer one, by the look of it. He peered at it closely. The hair, the finest gold wires he had ever seen; the bloom on the silver cheeks, like a butterfly's wing; the eyes, bright blue jewels, almost alive in the way they seemed to look at him!

Only Dr. Kalmenius could have created this. And he must have brought it for Karl. What did the figure do?

Karl reached out and lifted the prince's hand from his lap. With a little flicker of his energy, Prince Florian shook Karl's hand, and sang a bar of music for him. Karl's hair stood on end, for an idea had just come to him. Why not put this figure in the clock instead of Sir Ironsoul? It was more finely finished, and a handsome little boy who sang a pretty tune would be far more popular with the crowds than a faceless knight who did nothing but threaten people with a sword.

And then he could keep Sir Ironsoul for himself.

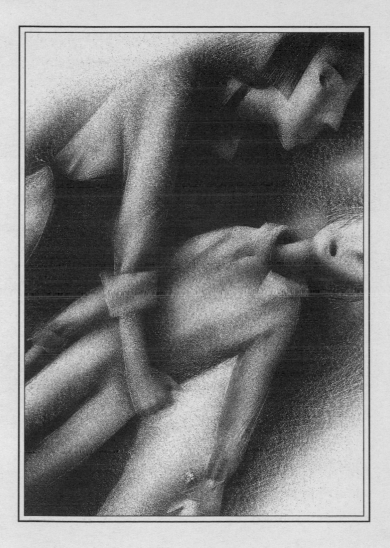

. . . an idea had just come to him.

And then. . . . Oh, how his mind raced. He could travel the world. He could become famous giving exhibitions and demonstrations.

He became quite dizzy as he thought of the uses to which he could put the metal knight. The gold he could steal, the forbidden treasures that could be his, if he had a secret accomplice, like Sir Ironsoul, who could be relied on always to kill and never to give him away! All he would have to do was to trick his intended victim into saying the word *devil*, and leave Sir Ironsoul nearby to play his part. He, Karl, could be somewhere else entirely, playing cards with a dozen witnesses, or even in church surrounded by the faithful. No one would ever know!

So excited did he become that he lost all sense of what was right. The church, his father and mother and brother and sister, Herr Ringelmann, every influence for good he'd ever known was whirled away into the darkness, and all he could see was the wealth and power that would be his if he used Sir Ironsoul in that way.

Before he could change his mind he threw the canvas over the knight, tucked the stiffening figure of Prince Florian under his arm, and set off back to the clock tower.

Meanwhile, Gretl was struggling through the snow toward the house where Fritz lodged. She could see from the end of the street that all the windows were dark except one in the attic where Fritz often used to work throughout the night. She had to knock half a dozen times before the land-lady came grumbling to open the door.

"Who is it? What do you want at this time of night? Oh, it's you, child; what in the world are you after?"

"I've got to speak to Herr Fritz! It's very impor-tant!"

Mumbling and frowning, the old lady stepped aside and said, "Yes, I heard all about that business at the inn. Making up wicked stories! Frightening people! I'll be glad when he's gone. In fact I've got half a mind to give him notice. Go on up, child, top of the stairs and keep going. No, you can't have a candle, this is the only one I've got and I need it myself. You've got sharp eyes; make do."

So Gretl climbed the four flights of stairs to the top of the house, each one darker and narrower than the one below, and came at last to a tiny landing where a line of light glowed beneath a door. There she knocked, and a nervous voice answered:

"Who is it? What do you want?"

"It's Gretl, Herr Fritz! From the inn! I've got to speak to you!"

"Come in, then—as long as you're by yourself—"

Gretl opened the door. She found Fritz standing in the light of a smoky lamp, throwing paper after paper into a leather bag that was bulging with his clothes and books and other bits and pieces. A glass of plum brandy stood on the table beside him. He had already drunk quite a lot, by the look of him, for his eyes were wild, his cheeks were flushed, and his hair was standing on end.

"What is it?" he said. "What do you want?"

"That story you told us," Gretl began, but she got no further, for the young man put his hands over his ears and shook his head violently.

"Don't speak of it! I wish I'd never begun it! I wish I'd never told a story in my life!"

"But you've got to listen to me!" she said. "Something dreadful's going to happen, and I don't know what it is because you didn't finish writing the story!"

"How do you know I didn't finish it?" he said.

She showed him the sheet of paper she'd found. He groaned, and put his face in his hands.

"Groaning won't help," she said. "You've got to finish the story properly. What happens next?"

"I don't know!" he cried. "I dreamed the first part of it, and it was so strange and horrible that I couldn't resist writing it down and pretending it was mine. . . . But I couldn't think of any more!"

"But what were you going to do when you got to that part?" she said.

"Make it up, of course!" he said. "I've done that before. I often do it. I enjoy the risk, you see. I start telling a story with no idea what's going to happen at the end, and I make it up when I get there. Sometimes it's even better than writing it down first. I was sure I could do it with this one. But when the door opened and the old man came in, I must have panicked. . . . Oh, I wish I'd never begun! I'll never tell a story again!"

"Oh, I wish I'd never begun!"

"You must tell the end of this one, though," said Gretl, "or something bad will happen. You've got to."

"I can't!"

"You must."

"I couldn't!"

"You have to."

"Impossible," he said. "I can't control it anymore. I wound it up and set it going, and it'll just have to work itself out. I wash my hands of it. I'm off!"

"But you can't! Where are you going?"

"Anywhere! Berlin, Vienna, Prague—as far away as I can get!"

And he poured himself another glass of plum brandy and swallowed it all in one go.

So Gretl sighed and turned to leave.

At the same time as she was feeling her way down the dark stairs in Fritz's lodging house, Karl was going back into the inn. He had taken little Florian up to the clock tower and fastened him to the frame, ignoring the prince's helpless struggles and his musical requests for mercy. When morning came, there he would be, Karl's masterpiece, on show as everyone expected. Karl would receive everyone's congratulations, and his certificate of competence from Herr Ringelmann, and he'd be entered in the roll of master clockwork-makers; then he could leave the town and make his way with Sir Ironsoul into the wide world, where power and fortune awaited him!

But when he opened the door of the inn to collect the little knight and hide him in his lodgings, he felt a shiver of fear. He stood on the threshold, afraid and unwilling to enter. Once again he took no notice of Putzi the cat, who jumped down from the windowsill when he saw the door open. There's no need to be superstitious about cats, but they are our fellow creatures and we shouldn't ignore them. It would have been polite of Karl to offer his knuckles for the old cat to rub his head against, but Karl was wound up too tightly for politeness. So he didn't see the cat stalking in past his legs.

Finally Karl gathered his courage and went in. How still the room was! And how sinister that little figure under the canvas! And that swordpoint: how wickedly sharp! Sharp enough to have pierced the canvas already, and be glinting in the lamplight...

Some coals settled in the stove, sending a little flare of red out on the floor and making Karl jump nervously. The glow made him think of the fires of hell, and he sweated and mopped his brow.

Then the long-case clock in the corner began to whirr and wheeze, preparing to strike. Karl leapt as if he'd been discovered in the act of murder, and then leaned weakly against the table, his heart beating like thunder.

"Oh, I can't bear this!" he said. "I've done nothing wrong, have I? Then why am I so nervous? What is there to be frightened of?"

Hearing his words, old Putzi decided that here was someone who might give him a little milk, if he asked nicely; so the cat jumped up on the table beside him, and rubbed himself on Karl's arm.

Feeling this, Karl turned in shock to see a black cat who had appeared, as it seemed, out of nowhere. Naturally, this was too much for Karl. He leapt away from the table with an exclamation of horror.

"Oh! What the devil—"

And then he clapped his hands to his mouth, as if trying to cram the word back inside. But it was too late. In the corner of the room, the metal figure had begun to move. The canvas fell to the floor, and Sir Ironsoul raised his sword even higher, and turned his helmet this way and that until he saw where Karl was cowering.

"No! No! Stop—wait—the tune—let me whistle the tune—"

But his lips were too dry. Frantic, he licked them with a dry tongue. No use! He couldn't produce a sound. Nearer and nearer came the little knight with the sharp sword, and Karl stumbled away, trying to hum, to sing, to whistle, and all he could do was cry and stammer and sob, and the knight came closer and closer.

When Gretl got back to the inn she heard Putzi miaowing inside, and said as she opened the door, "How did you get in, you silly cat?"

Putzi shot out into the square as Gretl came in, and wouldn't stop to be petted. Gretl shut the door and looked around for the prince, but she didn't see him anywhere. Instead, a horrid sight met her eyes, and made her shiver and clutch her breast. There in the middle of the room stood Sir Ironsoul, with his blank helmet shining and his sword slanting down. He was holding it like that because the point was in the throat of Karl the apprentice, who lay stark dead beside him.

Gretl nearly fainted, but she was a brave girl, and she had seen what lay in Karl's hand. It was the heavy iron key of the clock tower. With her mind in a whirl, she was still able to guess part of what had happened, if not all of it, and she realized what Karl must have done with the prince; so she took the key from his hand and ran out of the inn and across the square to the great dark tower.

She turned the key in the lock and began to climb, for the second time that night; but these stairs were higher and steeper than those in Fritz's lodging. They were darker, too; and there were bats that flitted through the air; and the wind groaned across the mouths of the mighty bells, and made their ropes swing dismally.

But up and up she climbed, until she came to the lowest of the clock chambers, where the oldest and simplest part of the mechanism was housed. In the darkness she felt her way around the huge iron cogwheels, the thick ropes, the stiff metal figures of St. Wolfgang and the Devil, but she didn't find the prince; and so she climbed on. She ran her hands over the Archangel Michael, and in his armor he reminded her of Sir Ironsoul, and she took her hands away quickly. She felt up the side of a figure in a painted robe, and her fingers explored his face until she realized that it was the skull-face of Death, and she took her hands away from him, too.

The higher she climbed, the more noise the clock made: a ticking and a tocking, a clicking and

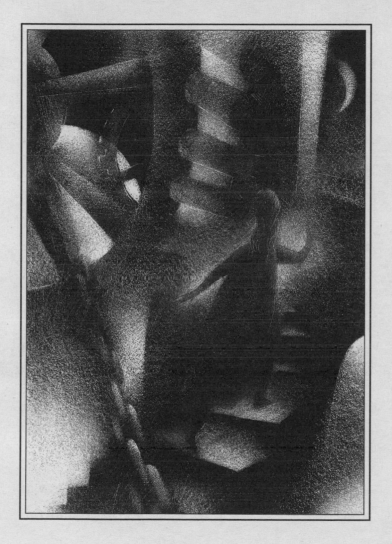

. . . up and up she climbed . . .

a creaking, a whirring and a rumbling. She clambered over struts and levers and chains and cogwheels, and the farther she went, the more she felt as if she, too, were becoming part of the clock. All the time she peered into the dark and felt around and listened with all her might.

Finally she clambered up through a trapdoor into the very topmost chamber, and found silver moonlight shining in on such a complexity of mechanical parts that she could make no sense of them at all. At the same moment, she heard a little song. It was the prince calling to her.

Dazzled by the moonlight, Gretl blinked and rubbed her eyes. And there was Prince Florian, with the very last of his clockwork life, singing like a nightingale.

"Oh! You poor cold thing! He's fastened you so tightly I can't undo the bolts—oh, that was wicked! He was going to leave you here and run away, I'm sure. What's the matter with you, Prince Florian? I'm sure you'd tell me if you could. I think you're ill, that's what the trouble is. I think you need warming up. You're too cold, but that's hardly surprising, seeing what they've done with you. Never mind! If I can't get you down, I'll stay up here with you. I can wrap my cloak around us both, you'll see. We're better off up here in any case, if you ask me. The things that have been going on! You'd never believe it! I won't tell you now, because you wouldn't go to sleep. I'll tell you in the morning, I promise. Are you comfortable, Prince Florian? You don't have to speak if you don't want to; you can just nod."

Prince Florian nodded, and Gretl tucked her cloak around them, and held the little boy in her arms as she went to sleep. The last thing she thought was: he is getting warmer, I'm sure; I can feel it!

The morning came. All through the town, visitors and townsfolk alike were getting dressed and eating their breakfasts hungrily, eager to see the new figure in the famous clock.

The snow-laden rooftops glittered and gleamed in the bright blue air, and the fragrance of roasting coffee and fresh-baked rolls drifted through the streets. And as time drew on toward ten o'clock, a strange rumor went around the town: the clockmaker's apprentice had been found dead! Murdered, what was more!

The police called Herr Ringelmann in to look at the body. The old clockmaker was appalled to see his apprentice lying dead.

"The poor boy! It was his day of fame! Whatever can have happened? What a disaster! Who can have done this terrible thing?"

"Do you recognize this figure, Herr Ringelmann?" said the sergeant. "This clockwork knight?"

"No, I've never seen it before in my life. Is that Karl's blood on its sword?"

"I'm afraid so. Do you think he could have made this figure?"

"No, certainly not! The figure he made is up in the clock. That's the tradition, you know, Sergeant: he was going to fit his new figure in the clock on the last evening of his apprenticeship, just as I did in my time. Karl was a good boy—a little quiet and morose, perhaps, but a good apprentice—I'm sure he did what he was supposed to do, and we'll see his new figure when it comes out in a minute or so. What a sad occasion, instead of a happy one! The new figure will have to be his memorial, poor boy."

Nothing was right that morning. The innkeeper was desperately anxious because Gretl was missing. What could have happened to her? The whole town was in a ferment. A crowd had gathered outside the inn, and they watched the policemen carrying out Karl's body on a stretcher, covered by a piece of canvas. But they didn't look that way for long, because it was nearly ten o'clock, and the time had come for the mechanism to reveal the new figure.

All eyes turned upward. There was even more interest than usual, because of the strange circumstances of Karl's death, and the square was so crowded that you couldn't see the cobbles; people were crammed shoulder to shoulder, and every face was turned up like a flower to the sun.

The hour began to strike. The ancient clock wheezed and whirred as the mechanism came into play. The familiar figures came out first, and bowed or gestured or simply twirled on their toes; there was St. Wolfgang, throwing the Devil over his shoulder; there was the Archangel Michael with his glittering armor; there was the figure Herr Ringelmann had made for the end of his apprenticeship, many years ago: a little boy who popped out, thumbed his nose at Death, and twiddled his fingers before ducking out of sight again.

And then came the new figure.

But it wasn't one figure, it was two: two sleeping children, a girl and a boy, so lifelike and beautiful that they didn't seem to be made of clockwork at all.

A gasp of surprise went up from the crowd as the two little figures yawned and stretched and looked down, clutching each other for fear of the height, and yet laughing and chatting together in the bright morning light, and pointing out the sights around the square.

"A work of genius!" cried the Burgomaster, and another voice said, "The best figures ever made!"

Then more voices joined in:

"A masterpiece!"

"Incomparable!"

"So lifelike—look at the way they're waving at us!"

"I've never seen anything like it!"

But Herr Ringelmann had his suspicions, and peered upward, shading his eyes. And then the innkeeper, looking up with everyone else, saw who it was, and gave a cry of joy.

"It's my Gretl! She's safe! Gretl, keep still! We'll come up and bring you down safely! Don't move! We'll be there in a moment!"

And very soon, the two children were safely on the ground. Two children, because the prince wasn't clockwork anymore; he was a child as real as any other, and so he remained. "The heart that is given must also be kept," as Dr. Kalmenius had been about to say to Prince Otto; but the Prince

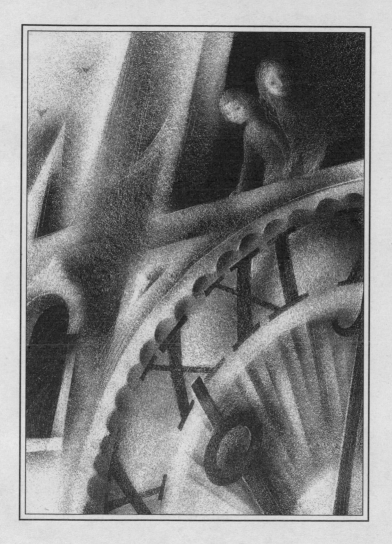

"A masterpiece!"

didn't listen, did he? No one could guess where the little boy had come from, and Florian couldn't remember. Presently everyone accepted that he had been lost, and that they had better look after him; so they did.

As for the metal knight with the bloodstained sword, Herr Ringelmann took it away to his workshop to examine closely. When they asked him about it later, he could only shake his head.

"I don't know how anyone expected that to work," he said. "It's full of miscellaneous bits and pieces, and they're not even connected up properly; broken springs, wheels with cogs missing, rusty gears—worthless rubbish, all of it! I do hope Karl didn't make it; I thought better of him than that. Well, my friends, it's just a mystery, and I don't suppose we'll ever get to the bottom of it."

Nor did they, because the one person who might have been able to tell them the truth was Fritz, and he had been scared so badly that he'd left town before the sun rose, and he never came back. He fled to another part of Germany, and he was going to stop writing fiction altogether, until he found he could earn lots of money by making up speeches for politicians. As for what happened to Dr. Kalmenius, who can say? He was only a character in a story, after all.

And if Gretl knew more than anyone, she said nothing about it. She had lost her heart to the prince, and kept it, too, which was how he came to be turned from clockwork into boy. So they both lived happily ever after; and that was how they all wound up.

THE END

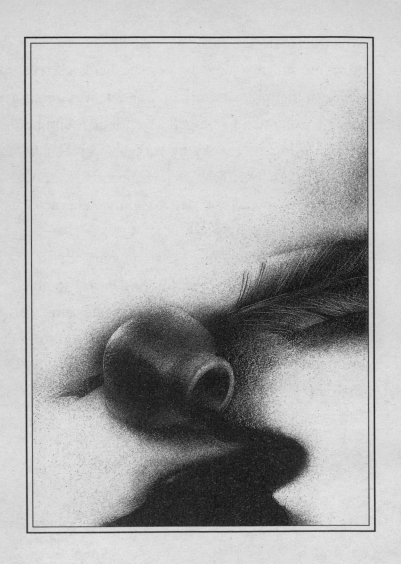

INDEX OF ILLUSTRATIONS

Frontispiece	*ii*
A Note About Clocks	*viii*
Part One	*xii*
The White Horse Tavern	2
The great clock of Glockenheim	6
Karl only scowled.	13
. . . the horses were mad with fear . . .	19
There was something uncanny . . .	25
On the threshold stood a man . . .	27
Karl gasped at the detail . . .	37
The sheet of canvas fell softly to the floor . . .	47
Part Two	48
Prince Otto and Princess Mariposa	50
He spun gold into filaments finer than spiders' silk . . .	55

To save his friends, he sacrificed himself.   64

. . . the dreaded symptoms returned.   69

Part Three   74

Gretl could only stare . . .   76

. . . an idea had just come to him.   83

"Oh, I wish I'd never begun!"   89

. . . up and up she climbed . . .   97

"A masterpiece!"   105

The End   108

AFTER WORDS™

PHILIP PULLMAN'S

Clockwork
or *All Wound Up*

Illustrated by Leonid Gore

CONTENTS

About the Author

Q&A with Philip Pullman

Q&A with Leonid Gore

How Clockwork Works

Excerpt from an Opera of *Clockwork*

After Words™ guide by Cheryl Klein

About the Author

Philip Pullman received the highest awards given for children's literature in England — the Carnegie Medal and the Guardian Children's Book Award — for *The Golden Compass*, the first book in the His Dark Materials trilogy. Its sequels *The Subtle Knife* and *The Amber Spyglass* were equally acclaimed, and *The Amber Spyglass* received the overall Whitbread Book of the Year Award — the first book for young readers ever to take the top prize.

Mr. Pullman was born in Norwich, England, and educated in England, Zimbabwe, and Wales, before graduating from Oxford University. His other books include the Sally Lockhart quartet (*The Ruby in the Smoke*, *The Shadow in the North*, *The Tiger in the Well*, and *The Tin Princess*); *I Was a Rat!*; *The Firework-Maker's Daughter*; *Aladdin*; and *The Scarecrow and His Servant*. He is the recipient of the Eleanor Farjeon Award for children's literature and the Astrid Lindgren Memorial Award. He makes his home in Oxford, England, where he writes in a shed in the garden behind his house.

Q & A with Philip Pullman

Q: *On your Web site, you say about* Clockwork, *"This took a lot of working out. I was looking at one of the old clocks in the Science Museum in London one day, and I thought it would be fun to try and write a story in which one part turning this way connected to another part and made it turn that way, like the cogwheels of a clock. And when it was all fitted closely together, I could wind it up and set it going." What was involved in the working out? What other directions did you explore for the story?*

A: It was just a matter of writing down the bits I could see clearly and then trying to make them join up. There were gaps, of course, so I could see where I needed a cogwheel or a gear train. Then it was just trying to make up bits that would do that.

Q: *Did you make up the tune that stops Sir Ironsoul?*
A: My son Jamie made it up for me.

Q: *Karl tells Fritz, "You don't know what it is to sweat and strain for hours on end with no ideas at all, or to struggle with materials that break and tools that go blunt, or to tear your hair out trying to find a new variation on the same old theme." Fritz reflects that he doesn't know what he's saying, for "stories are just as hard as clocks to put together, and they can go wrong just as easily." What stories have you had the hardest time putting together? How do you sense when a story is going wrong, and how do you get it ticking along again?*

A: *Clockwork* was pretty hard! It's hard to describe how you sense when a story is going wrong, but it's unmistakable. It's so hard that I once wrote an essay of six thousand words trying to pin down exactly where the sense of it comes from, and I still couldn't say. But you always know.

Q: *The narrator comments, "Fritz was an optimist, and Karl was a pessimist, and that makes all the difference in the world." Which would you describe yourself as?*
A: I like the phrase of the Italian political philosopher Gramsci: a pessimist of the intellect, and an optimist of the will.

Q: *Clockwork places a great emphasis on work: Karl is tortured because he has failed at his craft, and Fritz's work in creating stories inadvertently sets the rest of the plot ticking. What's your own attitude toward work? Do you love your job?*
A: Yes, I love it. I'm a follower of the Victorian sage John Ruskin in this. He thought that true work was where the human spirit was most fully and happily engaged. If everybody could feel that the work they did deeply and truly fulfilled every part of their interests and their talents, and that it was important work that was valued by the community they lived in, they'd all be a lot better off. It's one of the things I believe most passionately, and wish most deeply for the people I care about.

Q: *On your Web site, you refer to both* Clockwork *and* The Firework-Maker's Daughter *as "fairy tales" — a label that seems* *a little odd at first glance, as they're both longer and less straight-forward than what we conventionally think of as fairy tales. How do you define "fairy tale"?*

A: I call them fairy tales because — what else would you call them? They do belong together, and with my other two, *I Was a Rat!* and *The Scarecrow and His Servant.* What unites them, I think, is a tone of voice as much as anything else. There will be more of them, because I love telling stories like this.

Q: *The book has been optioned for film. Could you tell us where it is in development?*

A: That's precisely where it is: in development. "Development" is like a tunnel where you see things disappear at one end and then you lose sight of them till they come out the other.

Q: *What's your favorite timepiece?*

A: I am very fond of my gold Breguet watch.

Q & A with Leonid Gore

Leonid Gore was born in Russia. He studied illustration and graphic design at the Art School of Minsk and illustrated many books for children there. Since his arrival in the United States in 1990, he has illustrated more than twenty-five books, including *Behold the Trees* by Sue Alexander, *May Bird and the Ever After* by Jodi Lynn Anderson, *William Shakespeare's Hamlet* adapted by Bruce Coville, and *The Little Sleepyhead* by Fran Manushkin. He also excels at illustrations for longer works, including *The Christmas Rat* by Avi and *Voices of the Trojan War* by Kate Hovey, as well as book covers, including those for *Well Wished* and *The Folk Keeper* by Franny Billingsley, and *Blizzard!* by Jim Murphy.

Mr. Gore lives in Oakland, New Jersey.

Q: *How did you create the unique texture of the* Clockwork *art?*
A: I used black ink and black liquid acrylic over paper covered with textured acrylic gesso.

Q: *What's gesso?*
A: Gesso is similar to the acrylic paint used to paint houses. It comes in big cans, and you use it as background for paintings to be sure that the acrylic will attach to the canvas or the paper. When you paint over it, you can give a sense of a lot going on underneath the surface of the painting. With gesso you can scratch the paper, or clean it, or repaint it if you make a mistake.

Q: *Do you have a favorite artistic medium?*

A: I like to use pastel over watercolor paint. It allows me to combine the sudden natural effect of watercolor flow with the more defined and controlled pastel.

Q: *You have a very distinctive art style. How did you develop it?*

A: I love to try different styles and techniques, find something that fits or gives inspiration to me. Very often a new book project requires me to use something new. The trick is to find something I am comfortable with.

Q: *What's the difference between illustrating a picture book and illustrating a novel?*

A: In a picture book, the visual line is one of two voices telling a story. You, the illustrator, are truly a co-author. You can add some things that aren't in the text, create some details. The author's words and the illustrator's pictures work together, like when a choir sings with musical accompaniment — one isn't more important than another.

When I illustrate a novel, I am not able to tell the whole story through my paintings, so I try to set the mood of the story, to show settings and characters. It's more like decorating the story . . . you add music, but not all the time; you add refreshment.

How Clockwork Works

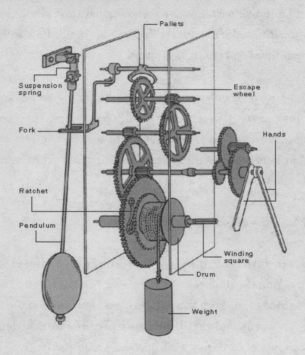

1. A clockmaker uses a key to turn the *winding square*, winding the rope (held steady by the *weight*) tight around the *drum*. (While the clock is being wound, the *ratchet* frees the drum to turn in the winding direction without moving the gears of the clock.)

2. The weight pulls the drum down and forward, which turns the gears and moves the clock's hands around its face.

3. The clockmaker sets the *pendulum* rocking back and forth. As it swings, it moves the *fork* and in turn the *pallets*, which catch and release the *escape wheel* one tooth at a time. The pallets alternately stop and free the movement of the gears and keep the weight from unwinding the drum all at once.

4. The rocking of the pallets pushes back through the fork, which, helped by the *suspension spring* and gravity, keeps the pendulum moving smoothly through its arc.

Excerpt from an Opera of *Clockwork*

In 2004, the Unicorn Theatre Company in London, England, produced a children's opera based upon *Clockwork* at the Linbury Theatre of the Royal Opera House in Covent Garden. The libretto was written by David Wood, with music by Stephen McNeff. At the beginning of the opera (excerpted here), the actors appear as figures in the great clock of Glockenheim. They soon change costumes to appear as Ringelmann, the Landlady, the Burgomaster, and other characters from the book.

For performance rights, please contact Casarotto Ramsay Ltd. at agents@casarotto.uk.com. Libretto © 2004 by David Wood.

The words in ALL CAPS are sung; the words in regular text are spoken.

Act I

(Short overture/prelude, during which the clock is revealed. Snow falls. Figures emerge.)

FIGURES: THE GREAT CLOCK
OF GLOCKENHEIM
TICK TOCK TICK
TICK TOCKING THE TIME

MECHANICAL MIRACLE
CENTURIES OLD
CLOCKWORK MASTERPIECE
A MARVEL TO BEHOLD

NEVER RUNNING SLOW
NEVER RUNNING FAST
HERALD OF EACH NEW DAY
WITNESS OF THE PAST

THE GREAT CLOCK
OF GLOCKENHEIM
TICK TOCK TICK
TICK TOCKING THE TIME

WITH A WHIRRING AND A RUMBLE
WE FIGURES APPEAR
TO SEE EV'RY ONE OF US
WOULD TAKE A YEAR
KNIGHTS ON HORSEBACK, SAINTS IN PRAYER
ANGELS AND THE DEVIL
AND DEATH WITH HIS ICY EYELESS STARE
WITH A WHIRRING AND A RUMBLE
WE WHIRL AND BOW AND GLIDE
WE ENTERTAIN THE CROWD
AND THEN TRUNDLE BACK INSIDE.

THE GREAT CLOCK
OF GLOCKENHEIM
EVER KEEPING TRACK
EVER TICKING ONWARDS
NEVER LOOKING BACK

THE GREAT CLOCK
OF GLOCKENHEIM
FINEST YOU WILL SEE
THE GREAT CLOCK
OF GLOCKENHEIM
PRIDE OF GERMANY

TICK TOCK TICK
TICK TOCK TICK
TICK TOCK TICKING THE TIME

(The figures move slowly in the shadows as Ringelmann and Karl enter downstage. Music continues. During Ringelmann's song, some of the figures exit into the clock.)

RINGELMANN: Well, my boy, your hour approaches.
The Great Clock awaits your handiwork.
Your apprenticeship will be over,
And you will be
A clockmaker like me.

AT TEN O'CLOCK TOMORROW
THE FIGURE YOU HAVE CRAFTED
WILL APPEAR ON THE HOUR
WILL APPEAR ON THE TOWER
AND YOU WILL FEEL PROUD
AS THE CROWD
CLAPS AND CHEERS
THAT YOU HAVE ACHIEVED
YOUR AMBITION
AND I WILL FEEL PROUD
AS YOUR TEACHER ALL THESE YEARS
WE ARE PART OF A PROUD TRADITION.

(Karl doesn't look pleased or proud, more sullen and nervous.)

Come, let's celebrate.
The White Horse Tavern awaits!

(Instantly lights up on the Tavern. Laughter. Drinking. We find the Landlady, Gretl, Fritz, and the Burgomaster, plus others. Cheers and greetings.)

LANDLADY: Welcome, gentlemen. Come and get warm!

RINGELMANN: Thank you. Thank you. Good evening, all!

BURGOMASTER: Ringelmann, old friend.
Come and drink some beer with me!

RINGELMANN: Burgomaster, I will!

LANDLADY: Gretl, serve the gentlemen!

GRETL: Yes, mother. On my way, gentlemen!

BURGOMASTER: And a mug for young what's his name,
　　　　　　your apprentice!

RINGELMANN: Karl. Join us, Karl. His big day tomorrow!

BURGOMASTER: Ah yes! The new figure for the clock!
　　　　　　I'll be there!

(Karl nods, expressionless.)

GRETL: Beer, gentlemen!

RINGELMANN: To Karl! To tomorrow! To success!

ALL: To Karl! To tomorrow! To success!

(All drink. Karl nods, but doesn't respond.)

FRITZ *(separated from the group)*: Karl, over here!
　　　　　　Come and join me, old fellow!

(Karl joins him.)

RINGELMANN: Fritz! Good evening!
　　　　　　Have you written a new story for us?

FRITZ (*waving sheets of paper*): Here, Herr Ringelmann!
　　　　　　Hot off the pen!

RINGELMANN: Splendid! I can't wait! (*to Burgomaster*)
　　　　　　Fritz tells a good scary story!

BURGOMASTER: Indeed!
　　　　　　THE LAST ONE GAVE ME SUCH A FRIGHT
　　　　　　I WOKE UP THREE TIMES IN THE NIGHT!

LANDLADY:
　　　　　　HE MAKES US HEAR THE SPOOKY WIND
　　　　　　WHISTLING THROUGH THE PINES
　　　　　　AND FEEL THE GHOSTLY FINGERS
　　　　　　CREEPING UP OUR SPINES!

BURGOMASTER:
　　　　　　HE KEEPS YOU TENSE IN SUSPENSE
　　　　　　TILL YOUR HEART STARTS TO THUMP
　　　　　　AND WHEN YOU LEAST EXPECT IT

GRETL:　　HE MAKES YOU JUMP!

RINGELMANN:
　　　　　　IT'S A SKILL, IT'S A CRAFT THAT I DEFINE
　　　　　　AS SOMEWHAT SIMILAR — TO MINE.

BURGOMASTER: Yours? But you don't tell stories!
You make clocks!

RINGELMANN:
A WELL-TOLD STORY'S
LIKE A WELL-MADE CLOCK
WITH INTRICATE COMPONENTS
THAT SUBTLY INTERLOCK
EACH CHARACTER A COG
EACH INCIDENT A SPRING
PERFECTLY ALIGNED
TO CAUSE THE PENDULUM TO SWING
A WELL-TOLD STORY'S
LIKE A WELL-MADE CLOCK
RELENTLESSLY UNFOLDING
TILL THE FINAL TOCK.